INTIMATE DIALOGUES

PROSE SERIES 83

Guernica Editions Inc. acknowledges the support of
The Canada Council for the Arts.
Guernica Editions Inc. acknowledges the support of
the Ontario Arts Council.

HÉLÈNE RIOUX

INTIMATE
DIALOGUES

TRANSLATED BY JONATHAN KAPLANSKY

GUERNICA

TORONTO – BUFFALO – LANCASTER (U.K.)

2008

Antonio D'Alfonso, editor
Guernica Editions Inc.
P.O. Box 117, Station P, Toronto (ON), Canada M5S 2S6
2250 Military Road, Tonawanda, N.Y. 14150-6000 U.S.A.

Distributors:
University of Toronto Press Distribution,
5201 Dufferin Street, Toronto (ON), Canada M3H 5T8
Gazelle Book Services, White Cross Mills, High Town, Lancaster LA1 4XS U.K.
Independent Publishers Group,
814 N. Franklin Street, Chicago, Il. 60610 U.S.A.

First edition.
Printed in Canada.

Legal Deposit – FourthQuarter
National Library of Canada
Library of Congress Catalog Card Number: 2008937334
Library and Archives Canada Cataloguing in Publication
Rioux, Hélène, 1949-
[Dialogues intimes. English]
Intimate dialogues / Hélène Rioux ; translated by Jonathan Kaplansky.
(Prose series; 83)
Translation of: Dialogues intimes.
ISBN 978-1-55071-295-7
I. Kaplansky, Jonathan, 1960- II. Title. III. Title: Dialogues intimes. English.
IV. Series.
PS8585.I46D5313 2008   C843'.54   C2008-905538-1

CONTENTS

1

VACATION

In August they are sitting on the balcony, each in their wicker armchair, a glass of pastis in hand. She sighs that summer in the city is just so grimy and noisy and what with them tearing up the streets it's *simply unbearable*.

In September he tells her that next summer he'd like to go windsurfing on a Caribbean island. She agrees – it's an excellent idea, though she'd rather try snorkelling. They say there are fish in the Caribbean that are incredibly beautiful or ugly. "But isn't summer the rainy season down south?" she remembers all of a sudden. "Dédé and Pablito spent two weeks in Guadeloupe last July and were invaded by tarantulas or giant beetles. Dédé was even bitten and had to be driven to the hospital. You can imagine the quality of care he received. Amazing that he pulled through. And he speaks Spanish." After a few minutes, his nose emerges from the newspaper. "One thing is puzzling me. Could you please explain what difference it makes that Dédé speaks Spanish? Guadeloupe is a French territory." She slams the bathroom door.

In October she confides that for years she's dreamt of touring the châteaux of the Loire valley.

He nods. "We could rent a car, there are those 'purchase and buyback' programs, you know. Very economical. One month crisscrossing France, eating in gourmet restaurants every night – wouldn't it be marvellous? We could stay with the locals. Rest assured, sweetie, we'd meet lots of interesting people." He shakes his head. Hmmm . . . staying with the locals – he isn't convinced. It's always very damp in those old houses. Besides, do they even offer comfortable beds? Because, if it means sleeping on a straw mattress . . . Whatever the case, all that rich food and those buttery sauces are not very good for his arteries. The last time he went to the doctor he was warned about high cholesterol. They'll think about it.

In November he intimates that France in August is crawling with German and American tourists. And the Japanese. There are endless traffic jams. "You're right, that kind of situation sounds awful," she concurs. "How about going in June?" But in June it's practically impossible to get away, he explains, the office is insanely busy. Besides, if they take their vacation in June, they'll still have to spend the rest of the summer in the city. She hadn't thought of that aspect of the question.

In December she suggests renting a house in New England. There are delightful fishing villages – her friend Maud showed her photos – where they could take part in all sorts of activities: swimming, hiking, deep sea fishing, mini cruises. She looked at a map; those villages all have names ending in Cove, Bay or

Harbor. She finds that so evocative, doesn't he? There are cafés and craft shops, little theatres. In the streets musicians play songs by Bob Dylan and Leonard Cohen. "A bit retro, you know?" He imagines the scene very well, and what's more, he has nothing against a bit of nostalgia.

In January, he announces that he's looked into it and that prices in New England are wild, especially now, with the terrible exchange rate. The whatchamacallit index just took a dive, he tries to explain, newspaper open to the financial section. As for the interest rates, no point in talking about them. In such circumstances the only solution is to tighten their belts. Wouldn't a cottage in the Laurentians be a more reasonable option?

In February she declares that she can't stand the mosquitoes and the noise from the motor boats. And besides, up north, all the lakes are polluted when they're not leech-infested. You can get all kinds of horrible illnesses: pustules, gastroenteritis, athlete's foot – to mention the least unpleasant. What's more, as he knows, she can't tolerate promiscuity. "I can assure you that nowadays the Laurentians are scarcely any better than trailer camping in Venise-en-Québec, if you get the picture. Apparently there they celebrate Christmas in the middle of July, with an outdoor midnight mass, and decorated Christmas trees – to give you an idea of the type of ambience. They even organize a potluck dinner with turkey and cranberry sauce." He points out that they are not obliged to attend.

9

But . . . no, she says. No, honestly. What she needs, personally, is a change of scenery.

In March, the economic situation improves and he suggests the Magdalen Islands. Another world completely. Beaches with sand as fine and white as flour, cliffs, escarpments, a lot of wind, very few hotels, and consequently, very little tourism. They could fill their lungs with pure air. And people speak with a truly exotic accent, evocative of old France, so to speak. She looks up: this possibility piques her interest. But is the car really in good enough shape to make that kind of trip, she wonders? "If we have to go by plane, considering the price of the ticket, we'd be better off going to France. Contemporary France."

In April, he changes his mind about the Magdalen Islands. Anyway, the water is freezing cold there and you can never be sure of the weather. She has made a foray into the travel agency. A dozen brochures about Greece are strewn upon the kitchen table. "Oh! A Mediterranean cruise! It would be like a honeymoon, hmm? Imagine the two of us on the deck of a ship, in our immaculate clothing, drinking ouzo in the sun. Eating olives just picked from the olive tree." He interrupts. "Olives, honey bunch, are picked in the fall and besides, freshly picked olives are inedible." What does he take her for? She knew that, she retorts, shrugging her shoulders. It was just a figure of speech. If a person can't speak metaphorically. He takes everything literally, which ends up becoming deadly . . . "At the ports of call, we could visit ancient sites," she continues after a moment.

"We would be learning and relaxing at the same time." Without completely agreeing, he implies that if he receives his bonus . . .

In May, she's leaning toward Portugal. "It's much less popular than Spain, you know. And the plane fare is much less expensive than Greece. Everyone says it's a country worth discovering. Walking in the footsteps of the great adventurers of the past, in fact, living out their adventure in the opposite way." But he maintains that air travel is perhaps too risky with this new wave of terrorism. An awkward silence – well, perhaps even a downright hostile silence. Once that's over, he points out to her that, in this case, "in the opposite way" seems a rather awkward turn of phrase. Did she mean "in reverse?" She leaves the room. She is fed up being treated this way. She meant exactly what she said.

In June he doesn't get his bonus after all. What about making a garden in the backyard? They could buy new chaises longues, an umbrella, and even a swing, why not? Some people claim that gardening is truly therapeutic. Tomatoes, fine herbs, annuals and perennials, he recites, eyes aglow. And morning glory along the wall. "We could picnic, while watching it all grow." He drags her along to a tree nursery to buy a variety of seeds and fertilizers.

In July all the neighbours are renovating their houses, the backyard is smothered in dust; they planted too late, nothing or almost nothing has grown, and the chirping of birds is drowned out by the noise of hammers, drills and electric saws. She groans that summer in the city really is *simply unbearable.*

In August, exhausted, they decide to try camping in the wilderness and spend a week at Lac Témiscamingue. It rains constantly. They are covered in blackfly bites and their sleeping bags smell of mildew. She catches an ear infection, while he suffers an attack of rheumatism that leaves him in terrible pain.

2

EATING OUT

"We *never* go out," she complains. "We really *should* go out, sometimes. After all, our vacation plans fell through. If we have to spend the whole year moping around this living room, I won't survive. I'll go nuts. I swear I'll *explode*."

He looks at her over his shoulder. He just got in from the office fifteen minutes ago, aching all over and vaguely depressed. He must be coming down with the flu. And that file on the refinery is going nowhere, in spite of all the effort he's put into it. This damn recession is killing every project with his work group.

"Of course, sugar. What are you in the mood for? The new Tavernier film is supposed to be . . ."

"Oh no! Not a movie! We spend enough time as it is in front of the television. I thought we could eat out somewhere."

Looking devastated, he answers that his mouth has been watering all day at the idea of eating yesterday's leftover stew — as far as he's concerned, it's even better the next day, the flavour of the broth is more intense. He even bought good sourdough bread to dip in the sauce, but eating out, in the end, yes why not, if she would like, he doesn't see why not. In fact, a few steps away, there's an Italian place just opened up on Fleury. It was written up in the newspaper last Saturday, got an excellent review.

She protests that no, if they're going to go out, there's *no point* in staying in the neighbourhood. It makes no sense. Besides, Fleury Street is ugly. She had been thinking of downtown.

But he's against the idea. He spent the whole day downtown, just returned from there. She should have phoned him this afternoon, he would have planned for it. Because she doesn't realize, but parking downtown is a whole production. You can never find a spot, and when you do, you need a permit, those public servants with all their crazy rules — parking lots cost an arm and a leg and parking in the street isn't safe. "In fact, only last week, Perron, at the office, had his car stolen one evening on Mountain Street. Didn't I tell you?" All in all, he thinks she's being a bit of a snob for not wanting to try a new restaurant just because it's on Fleury Street. He had no idea she found their area ugly.

She is incensed: she, a snob? Because she doesn't want to eat on Fleury Street? He doesn't understand a thing, or rather, he does, but, as usual, he pretends he doesn't. *He* goes out to work every day and sees people, while she spends the whole year at home, doing those ridiculous surveys, with only the telephone and the computer for company. It's only natural that she sometimes gets a yen to go out, and when that happens, she doesn't particularly feel like eating at an Italian restaurant in the neighbourhood.

14

Anyway, pasta isn't very inspiring. If she's eating out it's to try dishes that are too complicated to prepare at home.

They don't *only* serve pasta there, he breaks in. In the restaurant review the critic they raved about the veal scaloppini in Marsala wine. Served with roasted potatoes and an irresistible red pepper reduction, it seems. If she's not in the mood for meat, sea bream with olives is a specialty of theirs. She who loves olives. Picked fresh from the tree, he adds, sarcastically.

She smiles. The mood lightens. "Perhaps," she says finally, "but this evening I was thinking of something a little more exotic."

"What about Chinese then?" he suggests.

She replies that no, Chinese restaurants have got a bad reputation. "Do you know that they eat cats in their country? They sell them in the market, in cages, live. Dogs too." The thought of it makes her shudder, she says, shuddering. Knowing that they've already been suspected of capturing them here is enough to take away her appetite. She realizes she's prejudiced, but she can't help it. All things considered, she'd prefer Thai, or maybe Vietnamese.

He makes a face. "Vietnamese. I hope you're not planning on dragging me to Prince Arthur? It's so common around there."

"Now *you're* being a snob. Common, really! You must have gotten that word from some upper-crust British drama – no one around here uses it much. But if you're not in the mood for that, let's forget about exotic cuisine . . . Actually, the other day I passed a Russian place on Laurier. The menu was interesting: salmon Koulibiaca for me, chicken Kiev for you, caviar as a first course for us both. With sour cream and blinis. Unless you prefer borscht, I'm sure theirs is excellent – full of vitamins, you'll have a feast! We can wash it all down with iced vodka. The one with the cherry stems sends me reeling. For you I thought of another one, strong, flavoured with bison grass, designed for the Cossacks of the steppes of Georgia . . . And it said there were Gypsy musicians."

He answers, sniffing, that Russian food doesn't appeal to him tonight. Nor does iced vodka. He is coming down with the flu, so Gypsy music could give him a headache. Besides, the bill in that kind of establishment would be astronomical. The ruble may well have been devaluated, but caviar remains outrageously expensive. What if they went to a French bistro where they played Juliette Gréco or Mouloudji softly in the background? He's in the mood for simple, comforting food, a small steak, perhaps. Served with a good bottle of full-bodied Burgundy.

She doesn't look convinced. Where is this bistro, anyway?

On Saint-Denis.

"I thought you didn't want to go downtown. You're really being difficult tonight. Is it any easier to park on Saint-Denis?"

He thinks it over then suggests they go by metro and take a taxi home.

She shakes her head. The metro is out of the question. Then she says nothing. He is worried: is she sulking by any chance? She shakes her head. So he suggests that they discuss it quietly over a drink. *Fine*, she'd like a vodka martini. He opens the liquor cabinet. "There's no more vodka, sweetie pie. Shall I make it with gin?" No, he knows perfectly well that gin tastes like medicine to her. Her mother used to make her toddies with gin when she had colds as a child . . . It's coming back to her, Perron, that boor, finished the bottle of vodka the last time he was over at the house. "So, how about some vermouth? A glass of white wine? A kir?" he suggests. No, none of those appeal to her. Actually she doesn't want anything. "Are you positive?" All right, a glass of water, if he insists. He walks to the kitchen, opens a beer and brings her a glass of ice water with a maraschino cherry and a slice of lime floating on top. He sits down next to her on the couch.

She says they could leave the city for a change, and go, I don't know, to Sainte-Anne-de-Bellevue. It's not that far. They'd be sure to find a pretty restaurant there on the water. There are some there, in beautiful restored fieldstone houses, surrounded by weeping willows and apple trees . . . That way, they'd avoid the parking problem. "At this hour, sweetie pie? Think about it! Before we got there and were served, it would already be dark. Listen, I have a suggestion. Let's compromise. You want something exotic downtown; I'm in the mood to go out for Italian in the neighbourhood. So let's settle for an exotic place in the neighbourhood, or an Italian one down-town. What do you think?"

She sips her glass of water thoughtfully. "Actually, love, I think I will have a kir." While he's mixing it in the kitchen, she continues: "No, that's not the answer. Neither one of us will be satisfied. And I know you. If we go downtown, you'll be in a bad mood all evening. I won't enjoy my meal. And exotic restaurants in this neighbourhood are depressing. Two or three Ameri-can-style Chinese places with orange leatherette booths, paper napkins with all kinds of ads on them, and neon lights. We'll look like two zombies. And all their dishes are swimming in sickeningly sweet sauces, filled with empty calories and bad cholesterol."

He brings her the kir in her favourite crystal glass, featuring images that suggest cats.

"You didn't put in too much cassis?"

"No, sweetheart. I made it exactly the way you like it. Taste. I just had an idea: since it's so difficult to decide, we could put off eating out until tomorrow. Tonight I'll just go rent a video and we can order in chicken."

But she finds that chicken is too ordinary. This evening, she explains, she felt like living it up. She wanted to wear her new black velvet skirt, the one she bought in a second-hand clothing store last week. To be truly irresistible, she would have put on her leopard-print tights. But she may as well resign her-self: she'll break it all in tomorrow. "Tomorrow we'll eat out and you'll choose the restaurant," he promis-es, relieved.

"But this evening," he continues, "since you don't want chicken, we have to choose between pizza and Chinese and you don't like either."

"What about stopping in at a bakery and picking up a quiche on the way back from the video store?"

He approves. A quiche Lorraine and chocolate mousse for dessert. She'd prefer a spinach quiche and strawberry mousse – no, make it coffee.

Does she have a movie in mind? He feels a migraine beginning and thinks a comedy would relax him. She agrees, providing it's not an American film. Actually he had been thinking about *The Witches of Eastwick*. Jack Nicholson is really excellent in it. "Maybe," she says, "but we've seen it at least three times." No, either a French film or nothing. She's heard that *Amélie* is supposed to be funny.

"But sweetie pie, the movie is still playing in theatres. I'm sure it isn't out on video."

"In that case, let's go see it at the movies. You know, we *never* go out. Afterwards we could have a bite in a café. I've come across one that looks nice . . ."

3

THE PET

"Oh! If only I had a cat to keep me company!" she sighs. "I wouldn't be so bored. A nice fat cat that purred!" He raises an eyebrow without answering. It's Monday.

On Tuesday he answers that for some time he's found her rather silent. It seems as if something's eating her. What's going on? She answers that nothing's wrong. He insists: 'You're sure?" Yes, she's sure. Nothing's going on. Exactly. He says he doesn't like it when she uses that aggressive tone. Is it still because of that whole thing about the cat? She knows perfectly well he's allergic to cats. Is she trying to make him feel guilty?

Wednesday and Thursday pass by under a cloud in the rain. The delicate subject is carefully avoided. He comes home from work, she throws herself into hers. They pick at frozen food in strained silence. Later in the evening, he opens files, she goes to bed. Or vice-versa.

Friday, a lull. They make a date to meet at the movies for the 5:10 p.m. show. She wanted to see *La Féline*. He's left the car in the office parking lot. Afterwards they'll go eat at "Puss 'n Boots." If they have one drink too many, they'll take a taxi home.

She explains to him that the allergies are due to an enzyme, you know, in the animal's saliva. It seems there's a miracle product out now. "You brush it into the feline's fur and when he licks himself, the enzyme is neutralized, understand? Nothing to it." He shakes his head. "And the hair floating about in the air? It sticks to clothing. Have you thought of that? I don't want to waste a half an hour every morning brushing off my suits." "I promise you I'll vacuum every day," she reassures him. He looks sceptical. They wind up their evening at Katmandou.

Saturday, in the pet shop. He's stopped in front of the aquariums. "These tropical fish are simply splendid, aren't they?" She answers, "Yes, certainly, but the problem is that they don't purr."

Sunday arrives, treading very carefully. He mentions to her that it's all well and good, this distemper product whose praises she's been singing, but look, she's forgotten another aspect of the issue: the animal's claws. "Do you think I want to see all the furniture scratched? The carpeting ruined? Whereas an aquarium, with plants and multicoloured fish, would add a touch of elegance to the decor, don't you think?" She shrugs. Later, he tries to show his goodwill. "It's true that we could have him declawed . . ." he suggests, resigned. This drives her up the wall: "Never! That procedure is unnatural; I won't sink so low! A cat is not an ornament. I want a whole one, with fur and claws! Even neutering is out of the question." She opens a book, he makes coffee. "I find that it's also unnatural to keep an animal prisoner in a house," he declares. "A cat is above all a wild animal."

"Where did you come up with that? Cats have been domesticated since the time of the pharaohs. They were discovered in the pyramids, mummified."

Emerging from the shower, she says that it was never a matter of keeping their pet prisoner. They have a yard, right? "How will you like it when he does his business in the flowers?" he asks. "Nothing is more destructive than a cat's urine." Besides, if they allow him to go in the yard, they're sure to lose him. Everyone knows that cats jump over fences. Does she want to tie him up? She does not.

A new week begins and stretches out in interminable discussions on the advantages of tortoises, toy poodles, birds of the jungle and other creatures. Impossible to reach a consensus: she only likes cats. Parrots' piercing voices make her aggressive, poodles require too much attention, fish are heartless animals with no compassion who show no affection. And aren't turtles reptiles? At that rate why not a crocodile or a boa constrictor, to whom they'd have to feed live mice? Horrendous! She shivers in disgust at the thought.

Friday evening, he turns up with a large package tied with ribbon. "For you, sweetheart." It's a stuffed Garfield, life-sized. Thanks to the battery (not included), the cat emits various yawns and purrs. She restrains herself from throwing it in his face.

4

CHRISTMAS EVE

She's thought of something. This year, on Christmas Eve, she would like to have a few people over. He sets down his briefcase on the coffee table. He has just come in from the office. He answers that yes, it's an idea worth considering. November 24. There's still a good month left to organize it all.

The next day, he says he spoke with Perron and that, as it turns out, they have nothing planned for Christmas Eve. "We could concoct a nice little meal, a simple, elegant menu, poached salmon, perhaps. With beurre blanc or sorrel sauce. What do you say, honey bunch?" She makes a face. "The last time, remember, that idiot drank all my vodka," she replies He is surprised: it's unlike her to be vindictive. All their friends admire her heart of gold, concur that generosity is one of her finest qualities. So why attach any importance to the dregs of a vodka bottle? That incident occurred months ago. She explains that she had pictured something a bit more light-hearted, even exciting. She wanted to buy streamers, salsa and merengue CDs. So an evening with the Perrons is not exactly her idea of a celebration, she concludes. They're about as exciting as a rainy day. And even rain can be comforting at times. Especially on Sundays in autumn, with a cat purring by the fire. Diplomatically he decides to ignore this allusion. "What grates on me is that you men always end up talking shop," she continues. "And me, with . . . what's her name again? . . . oh yes, with Carole, we don't have much in common, you must have noticed. Once we're done exchanging recipes, we've run the gamut of conversational topics." The project is put on hold.

On December 3, she's more determined than ever. She definitely wants a Christmas Eve celebration, will not budge. With a lot of people. Look, she's made a guest list: Léa and Iaroslav, her new Bulgarian lover; Bernadette and her three children; Dédé and Pablito. And the Perrons of course, because it's important to him. He'd rather postpone the discussion until tomorrow. It's already after midnight; he is going to bed. Tomorrow will be a big day: he has to meet with the assistant deputy minister. If he manages to convince him, the office has a chance of scooping that fabulous contract. A few million are at stake, he specifies, which they certainly need. "Do you realize, sweetheart, that this meeting is a huge responsibility? The whole office is counting on me." She insists: she doesn't want to argue, just simply find out his opinion before sending out invitations. He assumes a rather doubtful expression. The group seems to him a rather odd assortment, he ventures. It's true, a single parent with her kids, two rather flamboyant gay men, a straight couple. "Léa is all right, but I'll bet that Iaroslav doesn't speak a word of French."

"You're wrong on that score, he's taking French courses for immigrants given by the government. Has the most adorable accent. How much did you say you were betting? . . . But enough chitchat. You want to go to bed, I know. So listen: I thought a traditional meal, turkey with stuffing, tourtière, fruitcake . . . Outrageously heavy, you'll say, and too much meat, but I say that just this once won't hurt. And a Christmas Eve like that would be a first for Iaroslav and Pablito. For Bernadette's children as well. We'd be like an extended family."

Since it is so important to her, he is not against it. However, he does think that she should also make a salad, perhaps citrus fruit, to serve in between the tourtière and the turkey, to lighten the meal. He quite likes pink grapefruit. Or else a tea-flavoured sherbet to help ease the digestion? If they are going to lighten the meal, she replies, they could replace the pork in the tourtière with chopped vegetables: leeks, carrots and turnips. He frowns; such a breach in tradition doesn't appeal to him In the least. Once they're at it they may as well swap the turkey for tofu. She scowls. He doesn't stand a chance of winning her over with that type of humour. From now on, she won't even bother to consult him if he's going to be uncooperative. He turns on the radio, she leafs through her cookbooks. A half hour goes by. She jots things down in a notebook; he turns off the radio and turns on the television to watch the news. During the sports broadcast, he thinks of something – an aspect of the reception that is bothering him. Has she thought of games for the children? If not, he's afraid that they'll be bored with all those adults they don't know.

On December 5, he says that he's thought it over, and doesn't find turkey all that appealing. They'll be stuck eating the leftovers for weeks. Why not choose a more original dish, guinea hen with Port, or Peking duck? She replies that the thought of cooking duck revolts her. The bird is too lovable, too endearing. And Peking duck, does he realize? It requires hours and hours of preparation. Will he even help her? And where are they going to find the guinea hens? Certainly not in the grocery stores in their neighbourhood.

Three days pass. She informs him that Léa has a depressed friend who is all alone for the holidays. Her husband has just dumped her. Her mother died of cancer last summer: first in the breast, then it spread. Her father, like most men, alas, quickly found solace; he is hibernating in Florida with a new fiancée twenty years his junior. And she has no children – a botched abortion left her sterile. He murmurs that, at any rate, the guy must be past the age of procreation. "I'm not talking to you about the fiancée. It's Léa's friend who is sterile. I suggested she bring her. After all, one more guest won't make much difference, there's always too much food. Okay with you?" He looks disillusioned. He has long since realized that whether or not it is okay with him does not carry a great deal of weight. She forges ahead. "Since we're ruling out turkey and duck, what would you say about a good beef stroganoff served with fresh pasta and snow peas that I'd set out, fan-shaped? I could place a sliced miniature tomato on each plate for colour. For dessert, a yule log, no, a chestnut mousse. In my cookbook, they call it a Mont Blanc. It sounds mouth-watering. Now there's a menu likely to please everyone . . . Do you have a suggestion for the first course?" He says no.

On December 10, he asks her if it wouldn't be better to have a buffet. "Everyone brings something, see? A lot less work for us." Out of the question. She'd been dreaming of a lavish meal with everyone seated at the table, candles in the middle, fine china, silver. It would be an opportunity to take her great aunt's service out of moth balls. They never use it. In any case, it grates on her to have to bring food when she's invited to dinner. "It was just a suggestion," he sighs. Because the idea grates on her, he comes around to her point of view.

Speaking of dishes, she saw a magnificent set of Limoges china in the window of the new antique shop on the corner. With tiny blue and yellow birds, a silver border. It would look really pretty on the damask tablecloth. "Shall we buy it? I asked – of course you'll shriek when you hear the price, but I swear it's reasonable. A real bargain, in fact, when you compare it with what they sell in the department stores. We could use it for the first time on Christmas Eve." But he thinks that with three kids at the table Limoges is just too risky. Even the damask tablecloth will get stained, he'll swear to it.

The next morning she looks absolutely shattered. "I've calculated. You know that with Léa's friend, we'll be thirteen at table?" He protests: that's all superstition. She doesn't wish to tempt fate, however. The same thing happens when she sees a ladder: she never walks under it, he knows full well. Only black cats pass muster with her. Thirteen at table, he's not seriously considering it! "One of the guests could die in the year. I don't want them to run that risk." He suggests nixing Bernadette and her children, who do not really fit in with that crowd, or else the depressed girlfriend whom, in any case, they don't know from Adam or Eve. Too late, she interrupts. Everyone's already accepted, all of them. No turning back now.

He leaves for work. She has about forty phone calls to make. A survey on what Christmas gifts are in that year. Coming home, he declares the problem settled. Stéphane breezed into the office, just back from his mission to Senegal and has promised to stop by on December 24. "Only for dessert, because he has to spend part of the evening with his daughter. But at least we'll be fourteen for a part of the meal. Happy?"

"Fantastic . . . We'll open the gifts over hors d'oeuvres. I just hope they'll think to bring some. Gifts, I mean."

Surely she is not intending to give to each of the guests a gift? This is the first he's heard of it. He finds she's going overboard. She will ruin them at that rate

She has already bought them, she tells him. At the Dollar King. Just a little something, purely symbolic, to put under the tree, to make it gay . . . "You know that some men still like to receive ties? But most spoke of computer games and CDs. And the women are divided between bath products and exotic cookbooks. Discouraging, isn't it, such a lack of originality?"

He remains dumbfounded.

It doesn't matter if he bought her bubble bath, like last year, she reassures him, seeing his dismay. She forgives him in advance. Deep down, she's not original as all that. To even the score, she'll give him a tie. A macrame tie.

Speaking of cookbooks, she found a recipe for Christmas punch. Vodka, cranberry juice and grenadine. Add three drops of Cointreau, garnish with orange slices and voilà! He is less than thrilled. "People always get sick from that sweet stuff."

Two problems arise on December 15. She has learned that Léa's girlfriend is vegetarian. They will have to reset the menu. And he just remembered that the Perrons are extremely intolerant of smokers. "We can't very well send Léa to the balcony to smoke her Gauloises! And Pablito, with his cigarillos! And even you smoke like a chimney at that type of occasion." He's afraid the evening will turn sour. She too. Besides, Perron always makes unpleasant sexist jokes after he's had one drink too many. Bernadette will be ready to scratch his eyes out, no doubt. He grumbles that he doesn't really find radical feminists much funnier. Not surprising that her husband took off. "She was never married," she retorts, a hint of impatience in her voice. "Each of the three children

29

was sired by someone else. I just hope you don't put your foot in your mouth on December 24." Sired, really! He raises his arms! If there is one word he can't stand, that's it.

The next day she asks if chestnuts are considered as nuts. "Because Fanny is allergic."

"Who's Fanny?" he asks. "A new guest?"

"Bernadette's youngest, you know very well, darling. All in all, I think I'd rather make a yule log, no, a chocolate fondue. Everyone likes that."

On December 20, she buys a Lampe Berger that absorbs the smoke. A genuine one. The oil releases a light fragrance of cinnamon – it smells like Christmas. She hopes the Perrons will display a minimum of tolerance. He tells her not to worry. "Everything will be fine, you'll see. I have faith." As for the menu, he suggests two lasagnas, one for meat-eaters, the other for vegetarians. That's an idea, she approves without too much enthusiasm. As for dessert, he warns her to be careful with chocolate. Certain brands contain traces of nuts. She'd better read the list of ingredients carefully. Come to think of it, a yule log wouldn't be a bad idea either, he says. They could even order it. He thinks that the baker at the corner must make excellent ones. She hadn't thought of it, but he's right, the dessert was like a thorn in her side. She'll take care of it tomorrow morning. "One problem solved," she sighs, relieved.

On the evening of December 23, the phone rings. "You'll be pleased," he says, after hanging up. "Perron has cancelled. His mother-in-law had an attack and is in a coma. She's in the hospital in Alma in intensive care. They have to leave immediately." Oh, but that doesn't suit her at all, because in the end Stéphane decided to bring his daughter "So?" he is surprised.

"So if the Perrons don't come, with Stéphane's daughter, we'll end up being thirteen at table."

He says he can't take it anymore. She herself is on the point of cancelling everything.

On December 24 at ten in the morning, in an aisle in the grocery store, she has a brainwave. "Roméo!" she cries. He stops pushing the cart, and looks at her, taken aback. "Roméo?"

"Yes, Roméo, you know, Dédé's dog."

"You don't really intend to feed that insufferable poodle at the table?" he counters.

"What do you mean, insufferable? I thought you liked poodles. And Roméo is very well-mannered. Admit it would be fun."

But he digs in his heels: if she invites that dog, he'll go eat in a restaurant. Without a reservation? On Christmas Eve? She finds him rather optimistic.

"Roméo will eat the first course with us at the table, then we'll put him in the manger" she suggests, to mollify him. "He can play the sheep."

"What manger?"

"Well, it's simple. You'll just have to make one while I make the cranberry punch."

5

VACATION (TAKE 2)

He sets the newspaper down on the coffee table. He says that, as their last vacation fell through, they could perhaps treat themselves to a week down South, in February. "Are you serious?" She is surprised. He answers that he has never been more serious. He mentioned it at the office and seems it would not be a problem. The secretary will postpone his appointments. Perron has been briefed about the urgent cases and can stand in for him at a moment's notice.

"Where down South?" she asks. He says he doesn't know yet. The simplest place would obviously be Florida. A three-hour flight, a huge selection of hotels. The airlines are desperate for customers. It may not be ideal, perhaps, but . . . She agrees: it isn't ideal. But Florida is big, he insists. They don't have to go to Miami or Fort Lauderdale. He has heard of a place called Naples, on the Gulf of Mexico. It would probably be fun to explore that.

Naples . . . She remains silent for a few moments. Then she says that she needs a day or two to think about it. He asks her not to think for too long: they're going to have to make reservations. It's already January 5.

The next day, while they're having a drink before dinner – he brought home a bottle of Pineau des Charentes, she put some cashews in a bowl – she tells him that Dédé phoned. He wanted to thank them for Christmas Eve. Pablito adored Léa's new lover. Incredibly charming, both exuberant and melancholy, so touching – those were his own words. She shares his opinion: Léa has always been lucky with men. Dédé even seemed a tad jealous.

He finds this type of reflection on Léa's men unnecessary, he complains. Isn't she happy with him?

"Slavs have something unquestionably Latin, don't you think?" She continues cooing, very casually. He had never seen things that way, but, yes, now that she's talking about it, he has to admit that perhaps there is an indefinable something. He goes into the kitchen to uncork the bottle of wine to let it breathe. "The same taste for excess, and that's saying something," she continues. "On the other hand, Dédé found Léa's girlfriend a bit obtuse, euphemistically speaking. He said that when you're that depressed, you should stay home . . . By the way, he and Pablito are going skiing in the Alps, the first two weeks of February." He takes a sip of Pineau. "Did they win the lottery?" he jeers. She assures him that it's less expensive than people think. And winter sports are excellent for your health. A real tonic. More and more doctors are recommending them. To tell the truth, she's a bit afraid of being bored in Florida, with all those retired people.

They sit down to dinner. She's prepared escargots for the first course. "What's expensive, in the end, is renting the chalet," she continues. "But when you can share . . ." He dunks his bread in the parsley butter. "Absolutely delicious, honey bunch," he declares. "You've surpassed yourself. Just enough garlic. I admit it's a little hard on the arteries, but for this once . . ." She explains that she cooked this dish for him to enjoy. She learned that before being put into the pot the poor things fast for months. It's inhuman, what they put animals through. He nods his head in vague solidarity. All of a sudden his appetite seems to have shrunk.

As for sharing, he points out to her that Dédé and Pablito are not very inclined to do so. To think they both showed up Christmas Eve with a bottle of wine from the corner store. "And they spent the evening drinking our Bourgogne Aligoté. Personally I find that kind of stinginess insulting," he concludes. "Don't you?"

She doesn't see what was so stingy. Each person gives according to their means, that's all there is to it.

They were the only ones who didn't bring a gift, he insists. Unless she considers the lottery ticket the two of them chipped in for that didn't even win to be a gift. When your means are that limited, you don't go skiing in the Alps.

An awkward silence lingers.

He points out that he hasn't gone downhill skiing in ten years. He doesn't feel like breaking a leg and being immobilized for months. That's what happened to Perron's wife's brother last year. There is a right age for each thing. She says she hates it that he's always harping on this question of age. In any case, she's not yet of an age to play golf, she points out, her tone sharp.

The main course is a spinach quiche that he picked up at a gourmet food shop on the way home. "Just seeing its colour, I'll bet they made it with frozen spinach," she decrees with a frown. "Far too green to be real." He replies that, at any rate, in January fresh spinach is imported and is hardly any better. Local is impossible to find. "Imagine our ancestors spending their long winters eating potatoes and turnips? You have to admit that we really are privileged." As they are discussing months of the year, he points out that he was thinking of leaving toward the end of February. The first two weeks it will be impossible for him to leave the office. Then he says that he had no intention of hurting her, earlier, by mentioning their age. In fact, he was speaking about his own. Contrary to what people may think, men age more rapidly and not as well as women – he read that in a scientific article. The proof: their life expectancy is ten years less. "Did I upset you, sweetheart?" She collects the plates. Then she asks him what he means by "contrary to what people may think." Personally, she has never thought otherwise.

The problem, she continues, while serving the salad, is that these days Florida has a bad reputation. Naive tourists are being attacked, cheated, stripped of their belongings, sometimes even killed. More and more you hear horror stories on television. "In fact, just the day before Christmas, the body of some unfortunate Quebec woman was found in a garbage bag on a beach. Well, what was left of her. I'll leave it to your imagination." But he doesn't want to imagine that type of thing, especially when he's eating. To change the subject, he tells her that he really likes it when she seasons the salad with lemon juice. So much better than even the finest vinegar. "I think like you do, sweetie pie," he continues, seeing she is not reacting. "There seems to be a kind of upsurge of evil. People seem to have gone mad – you ask yourself why. No place in the world has been spared. Should that prevent us from travelling?"

She asks him if he wants some cheese. He'd rather pass. The meal, while absolutely delicious, was rich enough with the butter from the escargots and the cream in the quiche. He'd be satisfied with a clementine. Since she has no cholesterol problem, she'll have a small wedge of Camembert. No, Roquefort. With a pear. She says they had Florida strawberries at the market. Huge ones, empty inside, flavourless. She didn't buy any.

They have their coffee in the living room, decaf for him, very strong for her with a lot of cream and sprinkled with cinnamon. On TV they're showing a documentary on allergies that she'd like to watch. He'll finish his crossword puzzle. "I can't help but think of that Quebec woman," she says, turning off the television right in the middle of the report. "Abandoned like that, in pieces, in a green garbage bag, such a cruel ending . . . The poor thing had probably dreamed of living it up, coming back tanned. Perhaps it was even the first time she'd gone away." He puts down his crossword puzzle. In his opinion, objectivity is key. "We don't know her story," he continues. "Perhaps she was travelling alone. Maybe she wasn't careful — she could have followed just anybody." In their case, there really would be no danger. He'd be with her, would protect her. But she has no interest whatsoever in being objective.

He suggests an after-dinner drink. There is that bottle of cognac that the Perrons brought on New Year's Day. They haven't opened it yet. Cognac makes her ill, she says. She'd prefer Cointreau, there's a drop left. "On ice, honey bunch?" As he likes, she likes it either way, will let him decide for her. This evening, she's really not inspired by that type of detail. Too trivial.

"It's better without," he says, bringing it over to her. "I don't know any other way to fully appreciate the flavour. Here's something to cheer you up, honey bunch." He sits down close to her on the couch, pats a cushion, distraught. It saddens him to see her so down. He says that it's normal to sink into depression in the middle of winter. Taking vitamins is all well and good, but the body lacks light. That's why he thought that a week in the sun would do them both good. She cannot actually believe that he planned on taking up golf. But he certainly doesn't want her to feel trapped, he assures her.

Later – they are at their third after-dinner drink and she is no less morose – she reminds him that *they* met in a bar. "So?" he asks, a bit taken aback.

"I followed you without knowing you."

He replies that he wasn't just anybody. "All the same," she says.

She feels feverish, will take a hot bath. He suggests he run it for her with her favourite foaming bath oil that he gave her at Christmas, the one with apricot flowers – but not too hot if she is feeling feverish. When she comes out of it, he is already in bed. He has taken advantage of this moment of respite to think. This once they could take separate vacations, he suggests. He'd go to Florida and she could ski her heart out in the Alps with Pablito and Dédé. They would meet up at the end of the week, feeling refreshed, ready to face the year's challenges. Yes, that's a possibility, she allows. They'll sleep on it. She'd rather not decide right away and then later regret it. She feels like reading for a while; this detective novel will take her mind off things. Given her frame of mind, he worries that that kind of writing could be too violent? She replies that she's not affected by violence in novels, but rather by the violent reality of the news. He places a kiss on her temple. She doesn't move a muscle, then turns a page. "How idiotic," she says. "I already guessed who the killer was." He turns out the bedside lamp on his side.

"Listen," she says the next morning, "I slept on it and it's a bit nuts to spend all that money just for a week in the Alps." If he's absolutely set on Florida, for this once, she'll compromise. As for him, given the before-dinner drinks, the discussions, the after-dinner drinks of the previous evening, he's gotten up late, doesn't even have time to drink a cup of coffee. He says they'll meet at five-thirty, at Katmandou. Then they'll re-examine their options.

Then, as usual, they spend the rest of January vacillating back and forth. One day, he has almost decided to go with her to the Alps. The next, he changes his mind. Or else she, despite all her good-will, cannot get used to the idea of Florida. Leaving one without the other does not seem an option to them. They try to reach a compromise: she suggests California, he suggests crossing Canada by train, but for the return trip, a week is not long enough. Besides, the train fare is a fortune. And the flights to California are all full.

When February arrives with its freezing rain, they're feeling increasingly feverish. The month is spent questioning: New York? Paris? Mont Tremblant? Guadeloupe (in the middle of winter there would be no risk of running into giant beetles)? Time passes so quickly . . . And then, too late, February has passed. When March arrives with its sleet, he can no longer get away from the office. She has five thousand forms to compile. She'll be busy at least until May.

What if they made do with a weekend at a hotel? There are enticing offers in the newspaper: getaway packages featuring whirlpool, massage, games room, healthy snacks, bottle of sparkling wine, fine-quality chocolate on the pillow. They'd have the impression of being somewhere else without even leaving the city . . . He comes up with this idea. She'd be more inclined to go to an inn with old-fashioned charm, in the country.

6

COLOURS

"I'm at the end of my rope," she cries, emerging from the bathroom – a genuine cry of distress, from deep within. "It's very simple, I just can't stand pale green anymore. Even thinking about it throws me into a depression – you can't imagine!" He'd been playing chess on his computer. He stops for a moment to remind her that barely three years ago they had the house repainted. Exactly, she says. Three years of feeling like she was in a hospital each time she took a bath was more than enough. If this continues, she'll end up in one. In the psychiatric ward. He'd been wondering whether if it would be better to move his knight or his rook and now he's lost his concentration.

He points out to her that, after all, they'd chosen the colours together. "People have the right to evolve," she cries, exasperated. Then she says nothing else. He then suggests continuing the discussion after he returns from Toronto. He's going to meet possible partners for the company's expansion project. His head is full of figures. For the moment, above all, he needs to relax. He'll only be away two days. She goes over to him and runs her hand through his hair. She understands the situation – she can wait. He moves his knight and the computer places his queen in check. Now he's discouraged. Given these circumstances he'd rather go to bed. She sits down at the dining room table to compile survey results.

"Have you thought of a colour?" he asks, returning home. The meeting with the investors went well: he feels buoyant. She answers that she's hesitating. "Caribbean jewel" coral is stunning, of course, but won't they tire of it after a few months? He agrees wholeheartedly. Coral, in the long run, could become irritating. A neutral shade would perhaps be a more suitable choice.

Later in the evening, she remembers a detail that bothers her: all their towels are white or beige, she says. So, if they painted the walls a neutral colour, as he suggests, well — the overall effect would actually be too neutral. It would affect their mood. And, he knows her, she likes cheerful surroundings when she's reading detective novels in the tub. He feels expansive — his stay in Toronto opened up delightful possibilities. "Why don't we replace our towels?" he suggests. "We could buy some in bright colours, which would contrast with the ivory walls." Hmmm . . . ivory, she's afraid it would be a bit pale, and therefore, show the dirt. Just by chance, she noticed a shade of creamy café au lait that would go perfectly if they decided to change the towels. He trusts her judgement. The only problem, she continues after a moment, is that they're high quality. Most of them almost new, she points out. It would break her heart to throw them out.

The next day she goes to the hardware store with Dédé. She no longer knows what to choose between "Sunday in May" blue and "baby's room" yellow. Either colour would be perfect. The bathroom glass and the soap dish are both black, so no problem on that score. However, while the leaf-patterned shower curtain matches the hospital green walls, with the blue it would surely be too dark . . . Incidentally, Dédé fell in love with the yellow. He bristles: personally, he is quite fond of blue. Come to think of it, so is she.

But well, this soft yellow really sends her. It's become imprinted upon her memory, as it were. How to put it – both frivolous and restrained. Baby, to sum up. She's brought a sample, would like him to tell her what he thinks of it. He looks at it carefully without managing to make up his mind. Now she's on a roll, and wonders if they shouldn't, once they're at it, repaint the kitchen. "It's time. And for once, don't contradict me." The kitchen? He frowns. And then: "Good idea, sweetie pie," he approves. The white has yellowed. I admit it's a bit sad."

Two days later he has weighed the pros and cons. In the end he finds this yellow a tad too dull. For a kitchen, he'd prefer something sunnier. After all, they spend quite a lot of time cooking – the room needs to be cheerful. He also stopped off at the hardware store on his lunch hour. Two other shades of yellow captured his attention: "daffodil bouquet" and "Seville saffron." But she's already bought the paint. She wanted to move quickly, as Dédé has offered to repaint. It'll take his mind off things, she explains. He's been on the verge of suicide ever since Pablito left during their ski trip, in February. She still can't believe that they broke up. She could have sworn that, beneath his offhand manner, Pablito was the more committed of the two. With men, you can never know. In the end, she should have gone to the Alps with them; perhaps she could have prevented the disaster. He interrupts: as far as he's concerned, it was high time those two separated. They could never agree on anything. In the long run, hearing them argue was becoming tiresome. She's forced to agree that on that score, he's right.

He wonders, however, if they shouldn't wait until summer before beginning the painting project. Right now, with the windows closed, he's afraid it would be difficult to breathe, especially for him with his weak bronchi. She understands the problem, but will Dédé still be free come summer? Will he even be around, she adds, her voice quivering. He thinks she has no cause to worry. She thinks the opposite. He says that you don't die from that. She looks at him, incensed: what about Romeo and Juliet? Phaedra? Camille?

A little later in the evening, she voices the idea that, since they'll be living in upheaval, they might as well take advantage of the situation to change the plumbing. It's all dilapidated. If they put it off till later, they are liable to have repainted for nothing. Initially he's not against this. But, for that type of work, he doubts that Dédé is qualified. Stéphane, in the office, has a cousin who specializes in renovations. He could ask him to come provide an estimate, and, if it's within their budget . . . She shakes her head. He insists: "Nothing's trickier than plumbing, sweetie pie. I refuse point blank to entrust it to just anyone." He doesn't understand, she says. Dédé is absolutely desperate. If it's going to be like that, she'd rather drop the whole project.

"In the end, perhaps it's not such a bad idea," she murmurs. They've been in bed for a good hour, but she can't manage to fall asleep. "What are you talking about, sweetie pie?" he mumbles, his voice heavy with sleep. She switches on the bedside lamp on her side. "Consulting Stéphane's cousin. After all, two opinions are better than one. And we aren't committing to anything by asking for an estimate . . . It seems to me we could also spruce up the bedroom. I don't know what got into us, painting it mauve three years ago. This time I'd like something soothing. Forest green, for instance . . . Are you sleeping already, my love?" He must be sleeping because he doesn't answer.

The next day he comes home from the office exhausted: the computer has broken down, the secretary had a dentist's appointment, left just after lunch and of course the telephone rang non-stop. All his files are late; he'll have to work for part of the evening. To further complicate matters, he spoke with Gaston, Stéphane's cousin, and he's booked until June, perhaps even later. It's always the same with those specialists – you have to reserve them years in advance. She looks every bit as shattered as

45

he. That rat Dédé, stopped by this morning to tell her he was leaving for Cuba. "To recuperate, can you imagine? What are we going to do with all this paint?" Seeing the kitchen cluttered with cans, bottles of turpentine and rollers depresses her. Him too. All they can do is take all that mess down to the basement to await summer.

7

HOBBIES

She's fed up watching television every evening, she declares. It's true, what else do they do? All things considered, they're like the majority of couples she polled in her latest survey: TV, food, computer, crossword puzzles. They really have to take up a hobby. Jazz up their dreary existence, get out of the day-to-day routine! Life is short: everyone knows that the day-to-day routine is not enough. Léa has begun taking belly dancing classes with Maud. She adores them. He raises an eyebrow. "Belly dancing? Do you see me performing the dance of the seven veils?" They don't have to do what Léa does, she says. That was just an example. Besides, belly dancing is for women only. But at the same school they also teach flamenco. And tango. It would be different. And they would meet people. She would like to expand their circle of friends.

It isn't that he's against the idea of a hobby. But social dancing, fox trots, tangos, polkas – no, really, she knows him, all that swaying just isn't for him. She nods her head: admittedly, he's a bit stiff, she assents. A little exercise wouldn't harm him. Dance, for example, could help him gain flexibility. He doesn't budge. She should suggest something else.

She asks him why it's always up to her to do the suggesting.

A few days pass. He mentioned bowling, which would have reminded him of when he was a teenager; beginner leagues exist, but she started to laugh. He did not press the issue. She mentioned language courses. One evening a week, the rest of the time, they would help each other. She'd lean toward Spanish classes, which would come in useful should they decide to travel to Latin America. He answered that after his exhausting days at the office, his mind would not be on studying. Besides Latin America was far from his first choice of travel destination. He'd far prefer Europe. Europe? But just last year he had found Europe to be terribly expensive, she said, feigning surprise.

In the Sunday paper, he spots an advertisement for an introduction to opera course. "Here's something out of the ordinary, don't you think? We know so little about it." "But do we really want to know?" she asks, rather absently. Seated at the kitchen table, she places her queen of hearts on his king of spades. He says she's being a bit of a wet blanket. She leaves her cards and goes back to bed. He pours himself some more coffee.

It rains all day. That evening, they order in pizza that they pick at in silence. At bedtime, they regret having wasted the Sunday. They could have, for instance, rented movies, played Scrabble, or dice. Or even made love – there are all those unorthodox positions mentioned in the Kama Sutra that they have yet

48

to try – the "dog," the "cobra," the "crab." Think of all those hours of sensual pleasure they have let disappear. They will never return, she laments. He is saddened as well. Especially with the completely ridiculous week ahead at the office, she has no idea. He'll scarcely have enough time to shave. They promise to learn to dialogue better.

The main problem with opera, she explains the next day, is that she's afraid of not getting along with other members of the group. Won't they end up with five or six rather reactionary old fogies, middle-aged women in mink coats? She explains that for her the goal is not just to go out for the sake of going out, but to add some spark, some imagination to their lives. If it's going to become a cause of conflict, she'd rather stay home.

Three days pass. In the evening, she reads books about cats. He listens to opera. On Saturday there is a lull: they go to the movies, but their hearts are not in it. He wanted a science fiction movie, she, a comedy. They end up seeing a historical blockbuster. Powdered wigs, minuets, hunting with the hounds on the moors. "What a dud! I yawned so much I thought I'd get lockjaw," she comments on the way out. "The actor who played the lead was totally unbelievable," he shoots back. "The actor? It's funny, I didn't find him that bad, but the crummy actress who played the marquise was overwhelmingly artificial. Where are the Jeanne Moreaus?" she exclaims. He replies that they're still out there, but far too old to play ingénues. The two of them wind up at Katmandou and continue their discussion about hobbies. New possibilities are explored, but none unanimously approved. Oenology? Too expensive. Volunteer work at the museum? Too stuffy. Rock climbing? A bit dangerous. An improvisation league? He believes that, unfortunately, they are too old for such diversions. She agrees.

Sunday is rainy.

Mid-afternoon, she has an idea: gathering mushrooms. Apparently they grow when it rains, and since it rains every Sunday . . . He looks up from his crossword puzzle. Without exactly saying yes, he raises no definitive objection. First of all, she points out, enthusiastically, they would learn to recognize them. Chanterelles, trumpet mushrooms, girolles, ceps, morels, boletus, meadow mushrooms, already the names are making her dream. With the best ones, they could prepare omelettes. "Imagine, my love, omelettes made with mushrooms gathered with our own hands in the undergrowth! If we're lucky, we may even find a truffle." Here is an argument that carries weight, he concedes, although regarding the truffle, he is sceptical: do they grow here? She doesn't know, but in the end, what does it matter? Such a hobby would allow them to go to the country more often, she continues excitedly. She loves walking in the forest. Come to think of it, so does he. He says that, what's more, their walks would be enriching. She adds that it suits all ages and budgets. For once, they agree: gathering mushrooms is the perfect activity. All they have to do is sign up with a group.

Tomorrow morning, she'll call the association of amateur mycology to obtain information.

But he is not sure he wants to pursue this activity with a group. They may end up finding themselves among militant environmentalists. He'd rather begin in a less official way, just the two of them, to see if they like it. In fact, next Sunday, if the sun deigns to show itself, they could go for a walk on the mountain. To find mushrooms you don't have to go very far . . .

8

KAMA SUTRA

Monday evening, in bed. "Kama Sutra is all well and good, but I'm not sure I agree with everything suggested there," she says, closing the book. "First of all, they divide women into mares, elephants and rabbits, and I don't see myself as any of those." He says that she's right: three categories is rather basic. Then he turns out the lamp; he's exhausted.

Tuesday morning, over coffee: "You know they suggest that men hit their women during lovemaking? With the palm, with fingers clenched, or with fist. I find these practices intolerable. They even describe the cries that should accompany the act. For example, I'm supposed to imitate a partridge moaning, a dove cooing, or, if it hurts too much, to cry 'Mama,' and you emit sounds like 'phut' or 'phât,' your mouth almost closed." He shares her view, described this way, it verges on the ridiculous. Then he takes his briefcase and kisses her on the temple: he's in a rush.

Late afternoon, at Katmandou, over drinks. "Some people have killed their partners with that kind of technique. They mention a king who, in the heat of the embrace, lost control of his dagger, and of another who poked out a dancer's eye." He nods.

Evidently, with a weapon in hand, love games may turn out to be dangerous, he agrees. Then he takes a sip of his amber beer; he's dying of thirst.

Early evening, in front of the television: "In India, oral love is called *auparishtaka* and is practised only by eunuchs, dissolute women and prostitutes," she says. He looks up. "Oh yes? I would have thought they'd be more open-minded." "There's a chapter on biting, and another on scratching," she continues. "Eight kinds of scratches, and each has a name, tiger's claw or peacock's foot, the jump of a hare or the leaf of a blue lotus. That's still the one I prefer, because of the image it evokes. They name the parts of the body to attack. They say that the impassioned man must not be preoccupied with the place where he inflicts the signs of his love. Because, in this story, it's always the man who attacks, evidently . . . Are you listening to me?" "Of course, angel," he replies. "Your book seems a bit sadistic to me." Then he returns to the television special on the consequences of the devaluation of the dollar; he is preoccupied this evening.

Late at night, she's in the bathtub; he's standing in front of the sink, brushing his teeth. "It seems that all parts of the body may be bitten, except for the upper lip, the eyes and inside the mouth," she says. "It gives me the shivers, really." He can't understand how you can bite someone inside the mouth – a rather acrobatic kind of kiss, isn't it? They're probably talking about the tongue, he supposes, and it's true that it must hurt. As for the eyes, it's funny, it would never have occurred to him. Then he goes to bed – the economic chaos disturbed him. Besides, tomorrow he has a rough day ahead.

Wednesday evening he comes home late for dinner. He stopped by the bookstore and found an illustrated treatise on sexual pleasure by Dr. Alfred B. Carnaby. It's easier to understand than the Kama Sutra, he believes. In any case, less muddled. And less violent. She agrees with him; all those practices are perhaps too exotic and do not really correspond with western customs. She suggests they consult the treatise together a little later. She grabs her coat and kisses him on the neck; she has a date with Maud at Katmandou.

Late at night, he's in bed with the treatise, she's just come in. "I began without you," he says. "The chapter on fantasies was interesting. It seems the average male reaches orgasm in three minutes, while the woman takes seven times longer, and even then, in order to reach it, she often has to imagine a muscle man tearing off her clothes. Is that true, honey bunch?" She admits that yes, sometimes, conjuring up some he-man can be arousing. "To delay ejaculation," he continues, the man concentrates on international politics or on multiplication tables." She replies that men are fascinating creatures. Then she hugs her pillow; she drank a little too much vodka with Maud and is exhausted.

Thursday morning, over coffee. He tells her that he read for part of the night, completely captivated. He learned a great deal. Did she know that horses, sheep, and camels masturbated? She was never interested in the sexual habits of four-legged creatures, she says, buttering her biscotte, but has long since known that men do so. In the end, all mammals resemble one another. He reproaches her for making fun of him, then goes to shave. She goes back to sleep; nothing really urgent to do today.

Later, at dinnertime. In the Kama Sutra, she read recipes for aphrodisiac potions, but the required ingredients are practically impossible to find here. "Cactus powder, monkey dung and I could go on." He thinks it's rather disgusting. The other aphrodisiacs involve names of plants with so many letters that she's unable to pronounce them. Just in case, she bought oysters. He's happy: he's crazy about them.

Later, at bedtime. She has also skimmed through the illustrated treatise on pleasure, she says. Her favourite chapter was the one on positions. She learned that certain positions are not recommended for men who are tired. The standing position, among others, is strongly advised against. He answers that in any case standing has never really inspired him. Then he swallows two tablets to prevent bloating. He doesn't know why, but the oysters are still sitting in his stomach.

Friday morning he doesn't get out of bed. Today he will take off, he's feeling great, wants to try one of those positions described in the treatise. The side position, it seems, offers numerous advantages to both partners. She agrees, the lateral position is marvellous. But this morning isn't good, she has about forty calls to make. Not easy to make their schedules coincide. She's sorry. So is he.

In the early evening, she went out shopping, has just come back. "Look what I found," she announces. Dice for playing Kama Sutra. The rules of the game are included. This will put us in the mood." But, in the end, he spent the afternoon consulting his files and feels the beginnings of a migraine. He doesn't really want to play.

Saturday at noon, in a restaurant. She declares to him that making love in a public place has always been one of her fantasies. She doesn't actually want him to fondle her here, in this crowded restaurant? She nods her head. He says that, personally, he'd like to do it outdoors, in nature, on a summer's day. She replies that in summer, in nature, there are too many famished mosquitoes. She suggests a beautiful autumn afternoon, on a carpet of dead leaves. Or in an orchard, with the scent of apples, would be intoxicating. Or else on the back seat of the car. Not very comfortable, he objects, frowning. He'd rather do it in the movies. As far as she's concerned, the movies are a bit conventional. All teenagers have done that at least once, hasn't he? She wonders how it is in an elevator. He wonders about doing it in the snow. The contrast between cold snow and the heat of desire. Yes, in a snowbank, she's titillated. They'll keep on their coats, mittens and tuques. They can't wait for winter.

Sunday, it rains. They'll stay in bed. Ventro-ventral, he suggests, obligingly. Does he mean the missionary position? Rather ordinary, she says. Besides, the illustrated treatise on pleasure doesn't really inspire her: too technical. She opens her Kama Sutra. The "cow?" No, she doesn't feel like grazing and mooing. The "crab?" He reads in turn. "You have to contract the legs and place them on your stomach. There's also the "splitting of a bamboo," or the "mare." With that you contract your *yoni*. But apparently this position requires a great deal of training . . ." She'd prefer more spontaneity, she explains. When you read these descriptions in a book, the whole enterprise always seems rather grotesque. What if they started by having breakfast? He's never very effective before he has his coffee. Nor is she. Besides, for making love, the bed really isn't the most original choice. A bit too conjugal, to her mind. "Can you imagine the number of couples, who, at this precise moment, are embracing in their bed, mechanically? Let's not do what everyone else is." The kitchen appeals to her. Or the bathroom.

9

ACTING OUT

"Do you realize, sweetie pie, that we've just experienced the last New Year's Eve of the millennium?" he sighs, conscientiously rinsing the last plate before placing it in the dishwasher. It is four o'clock in the morning on January 1, 1999. "That *New Year's Eve Special* was so boring!" he adds. "I didn't laugh even once!" She replies, yawning, that she's exhausted, is going to bed. Later, hugging the pillow, just before drifting off, she mumbles that they need to think of something out of the ordinary for next year. He agrees. He turns out the bedside lamp on his side.

"I'm fed up," she cries in February, furiously hurling her magazine onto the dining room table. "The media keep churning out stories of millennium bugs and other apocalyptic tales. They've spread the word. They're all alarmist, I swear! Incapable of seeing the magic of it all. Have we lost our sense of enchantment? Have we become so blasé? Personally, I see us as lucky to be able to experience this happening. But, of course, we have to prepare for the event. I'd even call it the Coming. The countdown has begun." That evening, he's immersed in his files. Besides, he's coming down with a bad case of the flu. So he really has no idea.

"Two hundred and ninety-two days, ten hours, fifty-seven minutes, three seconds . . . Do you realize, sweetie pie?" It is now March, an ugly Sunday with wet snow falling. He's sitting in front of the computer. She's lying on the burgundy couch, engrossed in Alberto Larrima's latest novel. She looks up. "What were you saying, sweetheart?"

"Two hundred and ninety-two days, ten hours, fifty-six minutes, seventeen seconds."

She returns to her reading. He to his calculations. "I think it's his most powerful work," she comments. "This time he doesn't beat around the bush. It sends shivers down my spine . . . Are you listening to me?"

"Fifty-five minutes, three, no, two seconds," he replies.

In April, she's the one with the flu. Wrapped in a down-filled quilt, she sips her hot gin toddy while he leafs through tourist brochures. "They're offering all sorts of enticing packages" he remarks. "What about going to Italy?"

"This summer? For our vacation? You're an angel. I've been dreaming of it for so long."

But no, she doesn't understand. He was thinking of an original way of marking the start of the year 2000. She makes a face. She's not sure that, for an event of this scope, Italy is the most original destination. Nor that he is the most adorable companion.

She wants to go off the beaten track, she announces in May. She's all fired up, as she is each time she returns from her monthly dinner in a vegetarian restaurant with her three high school friends:

one a belly dancer, another, Bernadette, a carpenter and mother of three, and the third a veterinarian. "Why not go to a place where the year 2000 doesn't create a frenzy?" she continues excitedly. In China, for example. Or in a Muslim country. No fuss? Is she sure about that? "Can you tell me why they'd celebrate the year 2000 in China?" she asks. "They reached it a long time ago. They're I don't know how many millenniums ahead of us." He shakes his head, then says he doesn't see the point in going to celebrate in a place where they don't celebrate. She calls him a conformist, a homebody, and slams the bathroom door. He turns on the TV.

"In any case, honey bunch, China is far too expensive. And in Muslim countries, there is always a risk of war. The Middle East is a powder keg. I thought of something: the Perrons made reservations in a small inn in the Laurentians. A show, champagne, a seven-course meal, door prizes. Would you like that?" But she's not thrilled at the idea of beginning the new millennium in the company of the Perrons. Especially since the last time they went to eat at their place she almost died of boredom listening to them talk politics. To find anyone more reactionary you'd have to be invited to the home of Jean-Marie Le Pen. Or to Stockwell Day's. And door prizes, what does that mean, in that kind of place? Phentex slippers? A macrame owl? "Or else they'll harass you to purchase a time share. I'm not convinced . . . In any case, it seems that you had to reserve last February for a room in any of the inns. It's now June 27. Isn't that a bit late?" He says that, because she finds the idea so unappealing, they should drop it. "Are you sulking, sweetheart?" she inquires after a half an hour.

In July, they spend a week in the Magdalen Islands. She's enchanted. So is he. On the third day, she declares it's the only place in the world where she'd like to be next January first. Not him. "Why not?" "Too cold." For the next four days, despite the sunshine, the lobsters and the sea, they sulk. Besides, she caught sunstroke and he got seasick during the fishing expedition. They don't even have enough of an appetite to appreciate the lobsters.

In August they patch things up and plan the most unorthodox escapades: eating seal at the North Pole in an igloo, fishing for alligators on a river boat on the Mississippi, drinking tea in the Sahara, coconut milk in Tahiti, receiving massages on the Fiji islands, climbing to the top of Mount Everest or the Tower of Pisa, parachute jumping in Mongolia, sleeping in an isba in Siberia, making love in a palace on the Riviera, in a dungeon, in a yurt, in an ahsram, being serenaded in Venice in a gondola, becoming engaged on a sampan on the Pearl River. "The sky's the limit!" she cries. "And this time, we'll be together." He's surprised: haven't they always been?

He wonders in September if New York wouldn't be the solution to their problem. "For starters, it's not far. We could go there by car. And Americans tend to be so expansive in what they do. I'm convinced that the celebration would be unforgettable."

"Expansive? Flashy, you mean? Tacky?"

He criticizes her for never wanting to do anything. She criticizes him for the same thing. For being contradictory. She says no.

In October, she declares to him that she never wants to hear the year 2000 mentioned again. Oversaturated, on the verge of nausea, of hysterics. After 1999, she plans on returning to 1998, that's it that's all. After all, it's only a convention, right? It's all so random. Just because some guy one day had the idea of inventing a calendar doesn't mean everyone has to conform to it. Being part of a flock was never her cup of tea. He chooses not to answer. She says he exasperates her when he doesn't answer.

November goes by without any other plans. He's involved with his files; she compiles her surveys. At the evening meal they avoid the subject.

Coming back from the office one evening in December, he finds her in tears on the burgundy couch. "Everyone's made plans," she sobs. "Maud and Gaston are going to New York, but all the hotels are full. They've been going out together for two weeks, did you know? It would have been so nice with them. Dédé is invited to his new conquest's place. Bernadette is spending the week at an outdoor sports centre with her children. They'll go snowshoeing, and sleigh riding by moonlight. Iaroslav and Léa have made reservations in a Russian restaurant. All the caviar you can eat, vodka, champagne, gypsy musicians . . . And us, we'll just end up like rejects, doing nothing." He brings her a kir in her favourite glass, featuring images of tiny cats. He takes her in his arms, caresses her hair, waits a few moments. "You'll never guess, sweetie pie, the inn where the Perron's had planned to go has burned down," he announces finally, triumphant. "Razed to the ground. We could concoct a little New Year's Eve celebration for four, what do you say? I've already thought about a menu . . ."

"When you think of it, sweetie pie, we've just experienced the first New Year's Eve of the new millennium . . . ," he says with a sigh, conscientiously rinsing the last plate before placing it in the dishwasher. It's four o'clock on the morning on January 1, 2000. "But that *New Year's Eve Special* was very well done!" he adds. "I laughed a lot. Didn't you?"

10

THE BABY

"We never really talked about it," he says "but don't you think it's time we thought about having a baby?" She agrees — it's an excellent way to begin the new millennium. It's January. If they made it now, the child would be born in the fall, which couldn't be better. With any luck, the happy event will take place during Indian summer. She's sure that being born during Indian summer is a good omen. The next day she goes to the library to look for books on astrology. "I've studied the situation thoroughly," she explains. "In our case Virgo or Libra are both compatible." He trusts her. But the problem is that she does not want to go through the final months of pregnancy in summer. The feet swell when it's hot and you can't get into a pair of sandals. Bernadette lived through that, and it's very uncomfortable. Did he know that pregnant women suffer more from the heat than others?

In February she says that if they do it now, the child will be born in November, which time-wise would be an advantage. "But Scorpio, with the two of us, is virtually incompatible. Perhaps we'd be better off waiting a few weeks before conceiving the baby. Might as well not take any chances."

The first two weeks of March she is terribly sick with the flu. Coughing fits, nasal congestion and aching all over: in those conditions, making love is the last thing on her mind. He catches the bug anyway and, for the rest of the month, it is he who's bedridden with a forty-degree fever.

In April, they're both better. The timing couldn't be better: the future child would be an Aquarius, a sign in perfect harmony with them both. But Bernadette pointed out to her that being eight months pregnant in winter is no picnic. "Can you imagine what it would be like putting on boots? And also I'd always be afraid of falling on the ice. I'd never dare leave the house." He agrees with her: better safe than sorry. They'll wait a bit still. But they do think it's too bad.

In May, they've decided: strike while the iron's hot. They try the positions recommended for fertilization in the treatise on sexuality: ventro-ventral "legs raised," ventro-dorsal "on the knees," and "X" position, even though few authors show interest in it.

In June, they've tried them all and nothing's happened. She contemplates consulting a fertility specialist. He deems there's no need yet for alarm. She criticizes him for always procrastinating. And he criticizes her for being too tense: "You are so stressed out that the sperm can't get through," he explains.

In July, she's thought about it: in her opinion, to facilitate reproduction, the surroundings must be favourable, which is not the case. After all, the little one to come must feel welcome. "What do you suggest? he asks. Prepare a nest for the baby. That is, repaint the guest room. There's that soft yellow she can't resist: two gallons of it have been sitting in the basement for ages. He answers with a sigh that it's not a bad idea, even if he had other plans for their vacation. "Oh, yes? What plans?" she asks. She buys curtains patterned with ducks, a child's bed, three pairs of pyjamas and a toy box.

In August, he gives her a book on names containing more than five thousand first names. Justinien, Chloé, Rodolphe, Adélaïde: they spend their evenings analysing the pros and cons of each. She quite likes Adélaïde, for the way it sounds, but according to the book it implies a difficult personality. "Its totem plant is the rosebush," she reads. "They say that Adelaide is both the flower and thorn." Edwidge and Philippine are temperamental, Félicie and Geraldine, narcissistic, characteristics they can't stand. Patricia is the scent of the earth, which is very pretty, but they don't like the name. Nor do they like Alphonse, even though he is described as a calm and thoughtful child. Baptiste's motto is "He who carries the world," which is after all rather cumbersome. As for Norbert, his totem animal is the grass snake, which is enough to eliminate a more exhaustive analysis.

In September, both of them are very busy.

In October, after spending a day at Bernadette's, she doesn't know if she really wants to have a baby. Even though she'd received all the shots, little Fanny caught the mumps and her son was caught smoking in the schoolyard. The administration is thinking of expelling him. And the elder daughter is anorexic. "If you knew how her children are worrying her, you would be wondering as well."

In November, it is he who's wondering: aren't they too old to procreate? She should think of how old they will be when the child's a teenager, with the problems that implies – drugs, dropout, delinquency and everything else. The very idea of this drains him of all energy. As for her, she's afraid her health isn't good enough to see her pregnancy through to the end. She'd not recover from a miscarriage. There's always adoption. China, Africa, Latin America: no shortage of choices. They promise to think seriously about it.

When December arrives, they find that, once again, the year has gone by very quickly.

Born in Montreal, Hélène Rioux has has published six novels as well as short stories and poetry. Nominated four times for Governor General's Awards, she has won the Grand Prix littéraire of the Journal de Montréal, the Prix de la Société des écrivains canadiens, the Prix France-Québec and the QSPELL award for translation. She is also a translator from English to French. She has translated fifteen novels by Lucy Maud Montgomery as well as works by Bernice Morgan and Yann Martel. She lives in Montreal and the Laurentians.

Jonathan Kaplansky has previously published translations of novels by Hélène Rioux, Hélène Dorion and Pauline Michel, as well as various biographies and a volume of poetry by Serge Patrice Thibodeau. He is currently translating a journal by Annie Ernaux.